All About Cats

First published 1998 by Beltz & Gelberg, Weinheim
This edition published 2022 by Macmillan Children's Books
an imprint of Pan Macmillan
The Smithson, 6 Briset Street, London, EC1M 5NR
EU representative: Macmillan Publishers Ireland Limited
1st Floor, The Liffey Trust Centre,
117-126 Sheriff Street Upper, Dublin 1, D01 YC43
Associated companies throughout the world
www.panmacmillan.com

ISBN 978-1-5290-8645-4

1 3 5 7 9 8 6 4 2

A CIP catalogue record for this book is available from the British Library.

Printed in China

Axel Scheffler • Frantz Wittkamp • David Henry Wilson

All About Cats

Macmillan Children's Books

Cats are . . .

Cats are sleek, and cats are slick.

They read, and do arithmetic.

Cats paint lovely pictures too,

In red and yellow, green and blue.

Cats are . . . Mischievous

Here's a trick all cats adore.

The thought of it will make them grin:

Burst a balloon with just one claw –

The dog will jump right out of its skin!

Cats are . . . Playful

Cats love playing games with a ball
Out in the garden or in the house.
But the game that they love most of all
Is the one called 'Catch a Little Mouse'.

Cats are . . . Hungry

Tummies are rumbling – time to eat!

And every single meal's a treat.

Each cat has its favourite dish:

Chicken, sausage, yummy fish.

Cats are . . . Sleepy

Tired cats sleep anywhere –
A floor, a stair, a mat, a chair.
Of all the places where they rest,
Cushioned sofas are the best.

Cats are . . . Loving

Parents always help each other -
That's what makes a happy marriage.
A kitten's carried by its mother,
While father wheels the baby carriage.

Cats are ... Collectors

If the tomcat's mood is good,

He'll sing and wander through the wood,

And catch a butterfly in his net,

And take it home to be his pet.

Cats are . . . Quiet

Father's catnaps are well known
There must be silence in the house.
The kittens sigh and roll their eyes,
But sit as quietly as a mouse.

Cats are . . . Grumpy

When the rain pours down from the sky,
Each cat would like to be home and dry.
They put up umbrellas and wear funny hats,
But the rain's still a pain for all pussy cats.

Cats are . . . Joyful

Birthdays are always a special treat.

They give the cats a good excuse

For scrumptious things to drink and eat,

Like fishcakes, milk, and rhubarb juice.

Cats are . . . Funny

The tomcat at the end of the day
Puts on a Punch and Judy play.
All the cats laugh loud with delight
When Judy Mouse gives Punch a fright.

Cats are . . . Musical

A love of music is characteristic

Of many cats, who are all artistic.

This one's a pianist – he's so clever,

The audience want him to play for ever.

Cats are . . . Clean

Every cat you've ever seen

Likes to be completely clean.

Every day, when cats go home,

They have a bath with lots of foam.

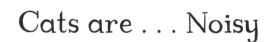

Cats are . . . Noisy

Cats love to sing – a beautiful sound! –
While the moon keeps smiling all night long.
The dogs sit listening on the ground,
Wagging their tails in time to the song.

All About the Creators

Frantz Wittkamp is a prize-winning German poet, especially well known for his poetry written for children. He is also an artist and a sculptor, with his own gallery in Germany.

Axel Scheffler is one of the world's most popular illustrators, best known for his collaborations with Julia Donaldson, including *The Gruffalo*. Axel's books have been translated into over 100 languages and his work has been exhibited all over the world. Axel was born in Germany and now lives in London.

David Henry Wilson is a children's author, best known for his *Jeremy James* series. As well as being an author and playwright, David has translated hundreds of books ranging from philosophy and art to children's picture books. He lives in Somerset.